Burke, Boykin & Company

Burke's Picture Primer

Spelling and reading taught in an easy and familiar manner

Burke, Boykin & Company

Burke's Picture Primer
Spelling and reading taught in an easy and familiar manner

ISBN/EAN: 9783337390846

Printed in Europe, USA, Canada, Australia, Japan

Cover: Foto ©Andreas Hilbeck / pixelio.de

More available books at **www.hansebooks.com**

BURKE'S

PICTURE PRIMER;

OR

SPELLING AND READING

TAUGHT IN AN EASY AND FAMILIAR MANNER.

WITH NUMEROUS CUTS.

[TWENTIETH THOUSAND.]

MACON, GEORGIA:

BURKE, BOYKIN & CO.

1864.

THE PICTURE PRIMER.

A	B
C	D
E	F

G	H
I	J
K	L

M	N
O	P
Q	R

S	T
U	V
W	X
Y	Z

ROMAN ALPHABET.

A	B	C	D	E
a	b	c	d	e

F	G	H	I	J
f	g	h	i	j

K	L	M	N	O
k	l	m	n	o

P	Q	R	S	T
p	q	r	s	t

U	V	W	X	Y	Z
u	v	w	x	y	z

1 2 3 4 5 6 7 8 9 0

C O M F R

T A N E D

W J S P U

B G H I L

X K Y Q Z V

---

d u c k i n g a b

e h x j m o q p

r f z l v t w y s

ITALIC ALPHABETS.—CAPITAL LETTERS.

A B C D E F

G H I J K L M

N O P Q R S T U

V W X Y Z Æ Œ

SMALL LETTERS.

a b c d e f g h i j k

l m n o p q r s t u v

w x y z œ œ

SYLLABLES OF TWO LETTERS.

Lesson I.					*Lesson II.*			
ba	ca	da	fa		ga	ha	ja	ka
be	ce	de	fe		ge	he	je	ke
bi	ci	di	fi		gi	hi	ji	ki
bo	co	do	fo		go	ho	jo	ko
bu	cu	du	fu		gu	hu	ju	ku
by	cy	dy	fy		gy	hy	jy	ky

Lesson III.					*Lesson IV.*			
la	ma	na	ra		sa	ta	va	wa
le	me	ne	re		se	te	ve	we
li	mi	ni	ri		si	ti	vi	wi
lo	mo	no	ro		so	to	vo	wo
lu	mu	nu	ru		su	tu	vu	—
ly	my	ny	ry		sy	ty	vy	wy

SYLLABLES OF TWO LETTERS.

Lesson V.				*Lesson VI.*			
ab	ac	ad	af	ag	ak	al	am
eb	ec	ed	ef	eg	ek	el	em
ib	ic	id	if	ig	ik	il	im
ob	oc	od	of	og	ok	ol	om
ub	uc	ud	uf	ug	uk	ul	um

Lesson VII.				*Lesson VIII.*		
an	ap	ar	as	at	av	ax
en	ep	er	es	et	ev	ex
in	ip	ir	is	it	iv	ix
on	op	or	os	ot	ov	ox
un	up	ur	us	ut	uv	ux

READING LESSONS.

Lesson I.

As I do it,
So do ye.
Is he up?
No. I am.
I am to do it.
It is to be so.
Is it to me?

Lesson II.

Do to us so.
No, I am to go.
It is my ox.
If I do go up.
I am to do so.
Be it so to me.
It is up in my

Lesson III.

Go in to it.
Am I to go in.
Ye go up to it.
If it be in it.
Is he in it?
No. He is on it.
It is to me.

Lesson IV.

Do ye so to me.
Or it is as he.
It is so. Do ye.
If I go, so do ye.
In it is all.
We do all of us.
An ox is in it.

READING LESSONS.

Lesson I.

Am I in
As he is
Ah to me
By my ox
Go in to
Do to us

Lesson II.

If we be
No, he is
To go on
Oh no do
No, if we
Up in it

Lesson III.	Lesson IV.
I am up	Be it so
So is she	As to me
Is it so	I do so
We go up	So do we
If he go	I go in
So do I	To do it

Lesson V.	Lesson VI.
If it be so	No, it is my ox
It is my ox	I am to go up
He is at it	Or is he to go up

Lesson VII.	Lesson VIII.
Do it to me	Is he to do it
It is by us	O no, I am to do it
Oh! it is he	To do it to us
I am to do it	Do to us the same
Do it as we do	Come up to me
It is to be so	He is to do it
No, it is up in it	May I do it now
Ah! no, it is by me	No, not yet

Lesson IX.	Lesson X.
Whip him well	What a noise
A good man	What is that
A bad boy	The ball room
A fine horse	That is my kite
It is very cold	Will you go out
How much is it	No, it snows
Is that all	What a fine ship

SYLLABLES OF THREE LETTERS.

Lesson I.

Ace	all	ass	bee	but	cot
act	and	ape	beg	bun	cow
add	ant	apt	bet	bug	cry
age	are	Bad	bit	Can	cub
aid	ark	bag	bog	cap	cup
ail	arm	bar	boy	car	cur
aim	art	bat	box	cat	cut
air	ask	bay	bow	cod	Day
ale	asp	bed	bud	cog	dan

Lesson II.

den	dot	egg	far	fir	fun
did	dry	ell	fat	fit	fur
die	dub	elm	fed	fix	fry
dig	dug	end	fee	fly	Gad
dim	dum	err	fen	fob	gag
din	dun	eve	few	fog	gap
dip	Ear	eye	fib	fop	gas
doe	eat	Fag	fig	for	gay
dog	eel	fan	fin	fox	gem

SYLLABLES OF THREE LETTERS.

Lesson III.

get	ham	hip	hut	jay	lag
gig	has	his	Ice	job	lap
gin	hat	hit	ill	jog	law
god	hay	hog	imp	jot	led
got	hem	hop	ink	jug	leg
gum	hen	hot	inn	Key	let
gun	her	how	ire	kid	lid
Had	hid	hug	Jam	kin	lie
hag	him	hum	jar	Lad	lip

Lesson IV.

lit	mar	mud	not	off	pan
log	mat	mug	now	old	pat
loo	may	Nay	nun	one	pay
lot	men	nap	nut	orb	pea
low	met	ney	Oak	ore	peg
lug	mix	net	oar	owl	pen
Mad	mob	new	oat	own	pet
man	mop	nod	odd	owe	pew
map	mow	nor	ode	Pad	pig

SYLLABLES OF THREE LETTERS.

Lesson V.

pie	put	ray	row	sea	six
pine	pug	rib	rub	see	sky
pip	Rag	rid	rug	set	sty
pit	ram	rig	rum	sex	sob
ply	raa	rim	run	she	son
pod	rap	rip	Sad	shy	sop
pop	rat	rob	sap	sin	sot
pot	raw	rod	sat	sip	spy
pry	red	rot	say	sit	sum

Lesson VI.

sun	the	too	use	way	wit
sup	thy	top	Van	web	won
Tag	tie	tow	vat	wed	woo
tan	tin	try	vex	wen	Yea
tap	tip	tub	Wag	wet	yes
tar	tit	tug	wan	who	yet
tax	toe	tun	war	why	yew
tea	tom	two	was	wig	yon
ten	ton	Urn	wax	win	you

B

READING LESSONS.

Lesson I.

A bad boy.
A mad man.
A fat dog.
We can mow.
So can I.
Can he hoe?

He is gay.
Eat an egg.
How hot it is!
A bee can fly.
It is a fox.
No, it is my cat.

Lesson II.

Do as you are bid.
I see you can run.
O yes! I can run, and I can hop too.
Get me the ink, and a new pen.
She is but one day old.
How can you say so?
Why how old are you?
He has a gun.

Lesson III.

It is in a box.
Get it for me.
May I go for it?
Go and get a bun for her.
May I eat it all?
Ann has a bat.
Bob got it for her.

READING LESSONS.

Lesson IV.

A man had a bad leg.
A boy has cut his arm.
Go and ask him how he did it.
The dog bit the cow in the leg.
Did you see the cat, how she ran up to the top?

Lesson V.

No, I did not see her do it.
The cow ate the hay.
Are you all up?
Yes, we are, all but Ann.
Go out and see the dew on the rye.
I got up at six, and Ned did so too.
But Tom did not; he was in bed at ten.

Lesson VI.

How can he do so to you and me?
Do not let the dog lie on the rug.
The pup can go by the van.
She can sew all day.
The boy Bob and I saw the old man and his son to-day.
I can let you go, if you do it.

READING LESSONS.

Lesson I.

A bad boy is a foe to God. Do not you be a bad boy. End not the day in sin, for it is bad to do so. Let not sin be in you, for men are too apt to sin. No joy is in the way of bad men. Run not in any ill way, for sin is the way to the pit. Can you do as I bid you? Do not act as a bad boy. Let me see you get up.

READING LESSONS.

Lesson II.

THE fox has got our fat hen. I can eat an egg. Tom, you can-not go if you cry. Let me get my hat to go. The cat and dog are oft at war. Why do you not go out in the air? If it is dry, I can go out to-day. Do not let a lie be in you. Pay to all men what is due. Can we not see the sun now? I can see the sky, but not the sun. The dog has bit our pig on the ear. Our old Tom cat has got a rat. Try and do all you can for the old. Do not bow but to one God

READING LESSONS.

Lesson III.

O let me be apt to do thy law, and fit me for thy way. The way of joy is the law to all who are not bad. His eye is on us all day. Woe is to the man who is bad. O, do not be bad or do ill, for God has set a day to vex all men who do ill. O God, may I set thy law by me, so as I may go in thy way. Let me not do ill, but fit me to die in thy Son. God is the joy of all who are not bad. Bad men do not do good.

READING LESSONS.

Lesson IV.

IT is the lot of all men to die: O let me not die in my sin; I can-not go to God if I do. He has no joy who is bad. If we sin we are not fit to die. In the way of sin is no joy. No one can see God; but his eye is on us all day. Let us pay to God his due, for he is the God of all men. Do not end the day in sin, for God has bid us not sin. The Son of God is my joy.

SYLLABLES OF THREE LETTERS.

The Vowel Long.

Lesson I.					*Lesson II.*		
bla	bra	cla	cra	dra	fla	fra	gla
ble	bre	cle	cre	dre	fle	fre	gle
bli	bri	cli	cri	dri	fli	fri	gli
blo	bro	clo	cro	dro	flo	fro	glo
blu	bru	clu	cru	dry	fly	fry	gly

Lesson III.					*Lesson IV.*		
gra	pla	pra	qua	sha	sma	sna	spa
gre	ple	pre	que	she	sme	sne	spe
gri	pli	pri	qui	shi	smi	sni	spi
gro	plo	pro	quo	sho	smo	sno	spo
gru	plu	pru	quy	shy	smy	sny	spy

Lesson V.					*Lesson VI.*	
ska	sla	sta	tra	wra	pha	cha
ske	sle	ste	tre	wre	phe	che
ski	sli	sti	tri	wri	phi	chi
sko	slo	sto	tro	wro	pho	cho
sky	sly	-·-	·--	··--	·h··	chy

SYLLABLES OF THREE LETTERS.

The Vowels Short.

Lesson VII.			Lesson VIII.		
a, short.			*e,* short.		
bad	can	had	bed	den	get
bag	cap	has	beg	hen	leg
bat	cat	hat	fed	men	let
fat	mad	rag	met	peg	red
lad	man	wag	net	den	vex
sad	mat	wax	set	pet	wet

Lesson IX.			Lesson X.		
i, short.			*o* and *u,* short.		
bid	did	fig	box	fog	fox
big	dig	fin	hop	dog	hot
bit	dim	fit	pop	rob	sop
him	lip	rid	pot	rot	top
his	pig	sit	bud	cup	but
hid	pin	tin	sun	mug	run

SYLLABLES OF FOUR LETTERS.

Lesson I.

Ache	been	born	cake	chip	come
arms	beer	both	calf	chit	cook
arts	bell	brad	call	chop	cool
Babe	bend	brag	came	chub	coop
back	best	bran	camp	clad	cord
bail	bill	bray	cane	clan	core
bait	bind	bred	cant	clap	cork
ball	bird	brew	cape	clay	corn
balm	bite	brim	care	claw	cost
band	blot	buck	cart	clip	crab
bang	boar	bulb	case	clod	crag
bank	boil	bulk	cash	clog	cram
bard	bold	bull	cask	clot	craw
bark	bolt	bump	cave	club	crew
barm	bond	burn	cell	coal	crib
barn	bone	bush	chap	coin	crop
base	book	bust	chat	coke	crow
bath	boot	buzz	chew	cold	cube
beam	bore	Cage	chin	comb	cuff

SYLLABLES OF FOUR LETTERS.

Lesson II.

curb	deem	dram	east	feet	fled
curd	deep	draw	edge	fell	flee
cure	deer	dreg	else	felt	flea
curl	dell	drop	etch	fern	flip
Dace	desk	drub	Face	fife	flit
dale	dice	drug	fact	file	flog
dame	dine	drum	fade	fill	flow
dane	dint	duck	fail	film	flux
damp	dive	duct	fall	find	foam
dare	dire	duke	fame	fine	foal
dark	dirt	dull	fang	fire	fold
darn	dish	dumb	fare	firm	folk
dart	dock	dung	farm	fish	fond
dash	doom	dupe	fast	fist	food
date	done	dusk	fate	five	fool
daub	dose	dust	faun	flag	foot
dean	dote	Each	fawn	flap	ford
dear	dove	earl	fear	flat	fork
deck	down	ease	feed	flaw	form
deed	drag	earn	feel	flax	fort

SYLLABLES OF FOUR LETTERS.

Lesson III.

four	gaze	gray	harm	hide	howl
fowl	germ	grim	harp	high	huge
free	gift	grin	hart	hill	hump
frog	gild	grot	hash	hind	hung
from	gill	grow	hate	hint	hunt
full	gird	gull	have	hire	hurt
fume	girl	gush	hawk	hiss	husk
fund	girt	gust	head	hive	Inch
fuss	give	Hack	heal	hold	itch
Gain	glad	hale	hear	hole	Jack
gale	glee	hair	heat	home	jade
gall	glen	hail	heed	hood	jeer
game	glut	half	heel	hoof	jerk
gang	goat	hall	heir	hook	jest
gape	gold	halt	helm	hoop	joke
garb	gone	hand	held	hope	join
gash	good	hang	help	horn	jolt
gasp	gore	harm	hemp	hose	jump
gate	gout	hare	herb	host	just
gave	gown	hark	herd	hour	Keel

SYLLABLES OF FOUR LETTERS.

Lesson IV.

keep	land	lime	lost	meal	monk
keen	lark	limp	love	meat	moon
kept	lard	line	luck	meek	more
kick	lass	link	lump	melt	moor
kill	last	lint	lurk	mend	morn
kind	late	lisp	Mace	mice	moss
king	lead	list	made	mild	most
kiss	lean	live	make	mile	mote
kite	leaf	load	male	milk	moth
knee	leap	loaf	mail	mill	move
knit	left	lock	malt	mind	much
knot	lend	loft	mane	mine	muff
know	lent	loin	main	mint	mule
Lace	less	long	more	mire	muse
lack	lest	look	mark	miss	musk
lake	lick	loom	mart	mist	must
lamb	life	loop	mast	mite	mute
lame	lift	lord	mask	mock	Name
lamp	like	lose	mass	mode	near
lane	limb	loss-	mean	mole	neat

SYLLABLES OF FOUR LETTERS.

Lesson V.

neck	pair	pick	pope	rain	rind
need	pale	pike	pore	rang	ring
nest	pall	pill	pork	rank	rise
next	palm	pine	port	rare	risk
nice	pang	pink	post	rash	rite
nigh	pane	pint	pour	rate	roam
nine	pare	pipe	pout	rave	roar
none	park	plan	pray	reap	robe
nook	part	plat	prim	rear	rock
noon	pass	play	pump	reed	rode
nose	path	plea	pure	reek	roll
note	pave	plod	push	reel	romp
noun	peck	plot	pull	rein	roof
Oath	pear	plug	puss	rend	rook
odds	peel	plum	Race	rest	room
pace	peep	pole	rack	rent	root
pack	peer	pomp	raft	rice	rope
page	pent	pond	rage	rich	rose
pain	pert	pool	rake	rick	rout
pail	pest	poor	rail	ride	rove

SYLLABLES OF FOUR LETTERS.

Lesson VI.

ruff	sect	shut	slut	span	sunk
rule	seed	sick	smug	spar	swan
rung	seek	side	snap	spin	sway
rush	seem	sift	snip	spot	swim
rust	seen	sigh	snow	spun	Tack
Sack	self	sign	snug	spur	tail
sake	sell	silk	soar	stab	take
safe	send	sing	soap	stag	tale
said	sent	sink	sock	star	talk
sail	sham	size	soft	stay	tall
sale	shad	skin	sold	stem	tame
salt	shed	skip	sole	step	tape
same	shin	slab	some	stew	tart
sand	ship	slap	song	stern	task
sash	shod	slay	soon	stop	tear
save	shop	slip	soot	such	tell
scau	shoe	slit	sore	suck	tend
scum	shot	slop	sort	suds	tent
seal	show	slow	soul	suit	term
seat	shun	slug	soup	sung	text

SYLLABLES OF FOUR LETTERS.

Lesson VII.

than	torn	twin	wage	went	wink
that	toss	type	wake	wept	wipe
thaw	town	Urge	walk	were	wire
thee	trap	Vane	wall	west	wise
then	tray	vale	wand	what	wish
they	tree	vamp	wane	when	wild
thin	triet	vane	want	whet	wolf
this	trig	vase	ward	whig	wood
thus	trim	vast	ware	whim	wool
tide	trip	veal	warm	whip	word
till	trod	vein	warn	whom	worm
time	trot	vend	wash	wick	wove
tint	true	verb	wasp	wide	wren
tire	tube	vest	wave	wife	Yard
toad	tune	vice	weak	with	year
toll	turk	view	wear	wild	yell
tone	turf	vile	weed	will	yest
took	turn	vine	week	wind	your
tool	tusk	Wade	weep	wine	Zest
tore	twig	waft	well	wing	zone

READING LESSONS OF ONE SYLLABLE.

Lesson I.

Now, Tray, stand upon your hind legs. What do you want? I know you want some bread and meat. There, now you may go home with Ann.

Lesson II.

I must not tell what I have done now. He could hear all that you then said. You must not stay at home this time.

Lesson III.

Where have you been to-day, George? I went out in the boat with John. Did James go out with you? We did not call to take him with us. That was not kind: why did you not?

Lesson IV.

The boy is gone to sleep. He ought not to do so at this time, for fear his sheep should go from him. But the dog will mind and watch them.

C

LESSONS OF ONE SYLLABLE.

Lesson V.

I should like to have a ride; when I am a man then I may.   Yes.   But you are too young now; you would fall off the horse's back.

Lesson VI.

Shall I come and play with you?   Yes, if you will be a good boy.   I will.   Let me come then. Will James come with you to-day?

Lesson VII.

BOYS and girls should not go out in boats, if they have not some one with them who can take care of them, and row well; for if they do, they will be sure to fall into some harm.   Now mind what I say; and then I shall love you.

LESSONS OF ONE SYLLABLE.

Lesson VIII.

Will you go with me? Shall Jane go? No.
She will cry. Let us not go fast. You are young.

Lesson IX.

John was so ill last night. What was it that
made him so ill? He had run in the sun in the day.

WORDS FAMILIAR TO CHILDREN.
Lesson I.
PARTS OF THE BODY, &c.

arms	cheek	hair	lips	teeth
back	chin	hands	mouth	thigh
beard	ears	head	nails	throat
brains	eyes	heart	neck	toes
blood	flesh	joints	nose	tongue
bones	face	knees	ribs	veins
breast	feet	legs	skin	wrist

WORDS FAMILIAR TO CHILDREN.

Lesson II.

TERMS RELATIVE TO DRESS, &c.

band	clothes	frock	lace	silk
boots	coat	gloves	pins	sleeve
cap	cloth	gown	ring	stock
clasp	curl	hat	shirt	string
cloak	dress	hose	shoes	thread

Lesson III.

TERMS APPLICABLE AT THE TABLE, &c.

ale	cheese	fish	pies	soup
beef	crumb	fowls	pork	stew
beer	crust	ham	rice	tarts
bread	ducks	hash	salt	veal
cakes	eggs	lamb	sauce	wine

WORDS FAMILIAR TO CHILDREN.

Lesson IV.

TO FRUITS, VEGETABLES, &c.

beans	grapes	limes	peach	spice
cloves	greens	mace	pears	stalk
figs	jam	nuts	peas	stem
fruit	leaf	oil	plumbs	tea

Lesson V.

TO A HOUSE, &c.

bar	door	lock	sand	straw
beam	floor	pane	spout	thateh
board	gate	paint	stairs	tiles
bolt	joist	roof	step	wall
brick	key	room	stone	yard

WORDS FAMILIAR TO CHILDREN.

Lesson VI.

TO FURNITURE, &c.

bed	couch	glass	mug	spoon
book	desk	knife	plate	stand
chair	dish	lamp	quilt	stool
chest	fork	mat	sheet	trunk

Lesson VII.

TO ANIMALS, &c.

ape	cat	ewe	mare	rat
ass	colt	foal	mule	sheep
bear	cow	goat	ox	snake
bull	deer	horse	pig	wolf

WORDS FAMILIAR TO CHILDREN.

Lesson VIII.

THINGS OCCURRING IN A FIELD, &c.

bark	dust	mud	road	vale
branch	earth	path	root	way
bud	grass	pool	shrub	weed
dirt	ground	plough	tree	wood
ditch	grove	rind	trunk	yoke

Lesson IX.

TERMS USED IN PLAY, &c.

ball	jump	play	sport	top
cry	laugh	roll	stick	toss
fall	leap	run	string	toy
hoop	peg	sing	throw	trap

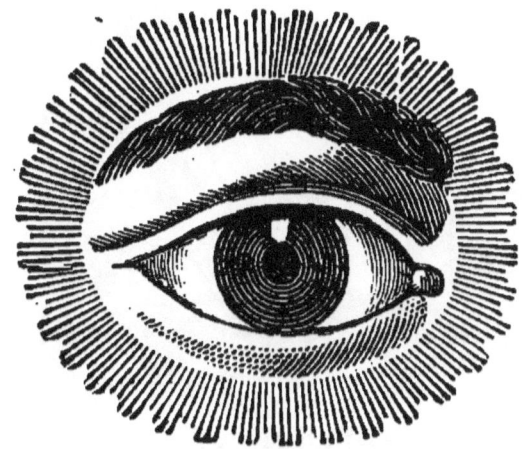

TERMS FAMILIAR TO CHILDREN.

Lesson X.

RELATING TO THE WEATHER, TIME, &c.

clear	day	month	rain	sun
cloud	hail	moon	sky	week
cold	heat	night	snow	wind
dark	ice	noon	stars	year

Lesson XI.

NUMERALS, &c.

one	five	nine	fourth	eighth
two	six	first	fifth	ninth
three	seven	second	sixth	once
four	eight	third	seventh	twice

SYLLABLES OF FIVE LETTERS.

Lssson I.

Badge	blind	brass	build	chest
baize	blink	braze	bunch	chine
baste	bliss	brawl	burst	chink
batch	bloat	brawn	Carve	chirp
bathe	block	bread	catch	choir
beard	blood	break	cause	choke
beast	bloom	bribe	cease	chuck
belle	bluff	brick	chafe	churl
bench	blunt	brief	chaff	churn
birch	blush	brine	chain	clack
birth	board	bring	chair	claim
black	boast	brink	chalk	clank
blade	booth	brisk	charm	clash
blame	botch	broad	chart	clasp
blank	bough	broil	chase	class
blast	bound	brook	cheap	clean
blaze	bourn	broth	cheat	clear
bleak	brace	broom	check	clerk
bleat	braid	brown	cheek	click
blend	brain	brute	cheer	climb
bless	brand	budge	chess	cling

SYLLABLES OF FIVE LETTERS.

Lesson 11.

cloak	cross	Faint	front	greet
clock	croup	false	frost	grief
close	crust	fault	froth	grill
cloth	curve	feast	frown	grind
cloud	Dance	fence	fruit	groan
clove	death	fetch	Gaunt	grope
clump	dense	field	ghost	gross
coach	depth	fifth	gland	grunt
copse	ditch	fight	glide	guard
couch	doubt	finch	globe	guess
count	drain	flail	goose	guide
court	drape	fleet	gorge	guile
crack	dread	fling	grace	guise
craft	dross	float	grand	Harsh
cramp	drunk	flush	grape	haste
crash	dunce	force	grasp	hatch
cream	dwarf	found	grate	haunt
creep	dwell	frail	grave	heart
crest	Earth	fraud	graze	hedge
crime	eaves	fresh	great	hence
croft	eight	frill	green	herse

SYLLABLES OF FIVE LETTERS.
Lesson III.

hitch	meant	prime	scoff	sleep
horse	might	prong	scrap	slide
house	mince	prune	scrub	slope
Jaunt	mirth	purse	sense	small
joint	mouth	Queen	serve	smart
judge	Niece	quest	shame	smear
juice	nurse	quill	sharp	smile
Kneel	Ought	quilt	shave	snail
Lapse	ounce	Raise	sheep	sneer
latch	Paint	range	shelf	snore
laugh	patch	reach	shift	snuff
learn	peace	right	shine	sound
ledge	pence	roast	shoal	space
leech	pinch	rogue	shove	spare
light	place	rough	shrub	spawn
loath	plead	rouse	siege	spear
loose	plumb	Saint	sight	speed
louse	poach	salve	since	spell
lungs	prate	sauce	sixth	spice
March	press	scald	slain	spire
match	pride	scene	slash	split

SYLLABLES OF FIVE LETTERS.

Lesson IV.

spoil	swain	throb	truss	whisk
spray	swear	thumb	trust	whist
squab	swell	thump	truth	white
stack	swift	tight	twine	whole
stall	swing	tithe	twirl	width
stag	swoon	tooth	twist	wight
staid	sword	torch	Valve	witch
stair	Taint	touch	verge	worse
stale	taste	tough	verse	worth
state	taunt	trace	Waist	would
stead	teach	tract	watch	wound
steel	teeth	trade	weald	wrath
sting	tenth	trail	weigh	wreck
stone	theme	train	whale	wrest
stool	thief	trash	wharf	wring
stoop	think	tread	wheel	wrist
store	thyme	treat	whelp	write
storm	third	troop	where	wrong
stray	thorn	trout	which	Yield
strip	those	truce	while	young
stuff	three	trump	whirl	youth

READING LESSONS OF WORDS NOT EXCEEDING TWO
SYLLABLES.

Lesson I.

CAN you swim? No, I can-not. I
should like to go in-to the sea. Those
peo-ple do not mind the salt wa-ter, for
they are used to it. But I do. If you
go to the sea-side, you can be ta-ken a long way
out in-to the sea in one of the bath-ing ma-chines,
which are drawn by hors-es, and then the per-son
who be-longs to them will dip you in-to the wa-
ter; which will do you good.

READING LESSONS.
Lesson 11.

ERE are some sol-diers talking. What do you think of them? are they not ve-ry fine fel-lows? Look at their swords and spears; what is that mu-sic? That is a drum. Would you like one? Yes. But you could not play on it. I should not like to be a sol-dier, be-cause I should have to fight. I think it is ve-ry wick-ed to do so. Would you like to go in-to bat-tle and have your head cut off? No; but God will pun-ish them for their crimes, and all wick-ed peo-ple like them. Did you ever see any horse sol-diers? Yes, I saw a great ma-ny at the next town once, when I went to see my cous-in.

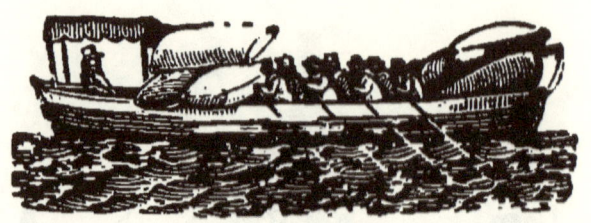

READING LESSONS OF WORDS NOT EXCEEDING
TWO SYLLABLES.

Lesson III.

ROW–ING aboat is hard work ; you see there are eight men row-ing : where are they go-ing in such haste ? Why, they are go-ing to the ships you see at a distance.

Lesson IV.

Two smug-glers have just land-ed some casks of spir-its, which they in-tend to dis-pose of with-out pay-ing the ex-cise duty. They are two very fierce and wick-ed look-ing men.

READING LESSONS OF WORDS NOT EXCEEDING TWO SYLLABLES.

Lesson V.

WHAT has the old man been doing? He has been get-ting some wa-ter out of the well; it is very hard work to draw the buck-et up when full of wa-ter. Chil-dren should nev-er go near a well; if they do, they are ve-ry like-ly to fall in.

Lesson VI.

DO you see that pleas-ure boat John? Ma-ny per-sons go on the wa-ter, and get some one to row them. You see they are cov-er-ed o-ver, to keep them from the wet.

Lesson VII.

JOHN, where do they grind corn? At the mill. It is then made into bread— bread is what we eat. The mil-ler car-ries his corn in his cart to the mill, where it is ground.

D

READING LESSONS OF WORDS NOT EXCEEDING TWO
SYLLABLES

Lesson VIII.

Are you fond of fish-ing? No; for it is cru-el
sport. I like to read my books, and to learn to
write.

Lesson IX.

GOATS are pret-ty crea-tures! What a
shame it is to make them draw a hea-
vy chaise. I am sure I would nev-er
ride in it, for if they can-not go fast
e-nough, their mas-ter beats them with a stick. I
have seen four chil-dren in a chaise, and the poor
goats al-most dead with fa-tigue! It is true, they
are ve-ry strong, but they are made to work e-ve-
ry day from morn-ing to night, and some peo-ple
do not half feed them.

Lesson X.

MA-RY, come with me, and watch
the cows quench-ing their thirst at
yon-der spring! I can-not tell what
we should do with-out them; for
cows, you know, give us milk, which is made in-
to but-ter and cheese.

WORDS OF TWO SYLLABLES.

Lesson I.

A bate	a lert	be bold	chis el
ab bey	a lone	be stow	ci der
a ble	al um	be youd	cir cle
a board	a miss	blem ish	cit ron
a bridge	a mount	bob bin	cit y
ab sent	an gel	bon net	clam our
ab sorb	an gry	bow er	clean ly
ac count	an tic	brave ly	cli ent
a cid	ap prove	brisk et	clo set
ac quire	a rise	bru tish	cof fee
a cross	ar rest	bun dle	co lon
ac tive	a side	bush el	come ly
a cute	as sure	but ter	com et
ad mire	at tire	Ca ble	com fort
a dopt	a wake	can dle	com ic
ad vice	Ba boon	ca ress	com ing
a far	bal loon	cat tle	com mand
af front	ban ner	cer tain	com mit
a gain	bare ly	chap let	com mon
a gree	bar ter	chat ter	com pare
ail ment	bear er	ches nut	com pel
a larm			com ply

WORDS OF TWO SYLLABLES.

Lesson II.

com pute	coun try	dew drop	em met
con ceal	cous in	dif fer	em press
con cern	co vey	di lute	end less
con demn	crab bed	din ner	en grave
con fine	crag gy	dis cern	en rage
con flict	cray on	dis close	en tail
con fuse	cre dit	dis course	en trap
con jure	crew et	dis grace	en voy
con nive	crim son	dis may	er mine
con sent	crook ed	dis pose	es cape
con sole	crys tal	dis tant	es tate
con sult	cul prit	dis tract	es teem
con tempt	cu rate	dit ty	e ther
con tent	cur tain	di vorce	e vade
con trol	dam age	do tage	e vent
con vey	dan ger	dow dy	e vil
con vince	dar ling	dri ver	ex act
cop per	de base	drug gist	ex cel
cor ner	de cease	dump ling	ex cess
cor rect	des pond	ea glet	ex cise
cot ton	de tail	ear nest	ex clude
coun sel	de tect	e cho	ex ert
coun tess	de void	em balm	ex ist

WORDS OF TWO SYLLABLES.

Lesson III.

ex pect	fo rage	glos sy	hun ger
ex pert	fore run	gos ling	hust ings
ex pose	for get	go vern	Im part
ex tend	for mer	grand son	in clude
Fa ble	for tune	grate ful	in fer
fal low	fos ter	gree dy	in sane
fal ter	fow ler	grit ty	in sult
far mer	fran tic	Hab it	in volve
fas ten	free man	hal low	it self
fat ten	fri gate	ham mer	Jas per
fee ble	frit ter	han dle	jes ter
fer ret	fru gal	hap pen	jo ker
fes ter	ful fil	har ness	jui cy
fes toon	fur nish	hat ter	ju ry
fi bre	fu ture	head long	jus tice
fig ure	Gal lant	hea then	Ken nel
fil bert	gam mon	hel met	kin dle
fla ky	gar ment	hid den	king dom
flat ten	gar ter	hi ther	kit ten
flim sy	gib bet	hog gish	kna vish
flow er	gin ger	hope ful	La bel
fod der	gleam ing	hor ror	la bour
fool ish	glit ter	hu man	lad der

WORDS OF TWO SYLLABLES.

Lesson IV.

lam poon	mal let	mur mur	pa per
lan cet	man kind	mush room	pa rade
land scape	mar ble	mut ton	par take
lap dog	mar-row	Na ture	pas sage
lar der	mar tyr	neck lace	pa tent
latch et	mas tiff	neigh bour	pat tern
la ver	mat tress	ner vous	pay ment
laun dress	max im	net tle	pen sive
law yer	mel low	neu ter	per ceive
lead en	men ace	nose gay	pes ter
lec ture	mer chant	nour ish	pew ter
lei sure	mes sage	num ber	pic ture
let ter	meth od	nut shell	pil grim
li bel	mid land	Ob ject	pim ple
lin en	mil ler	ob tain	pip pin
lin seed	mir ror	oc tave	pitch er
lis ten	mis deed	of fend	plain tiff
liv ing	mix ture	off set	plea sant
lock et	mod est	op press	plu mage
log wood	mois ture	or phan	poach er
low land	mon key	our self	pom mel
lum ber	moon light	out ward	pon tiff
Ma caw	mor tal	Pack age	pop lar
mag got	mot to	pal ace	post pone
main tain	moun tain	pan ther	pow der

WORDS OF TWO SYLLABLES.

Lesson V.

prac tice	reap er	sal mon	so journ
pre cise	re buke	samp ler	span gle
pri mate	re ceive	sau cy	spar row
pro ceed	re cline	saw dust	spell ing
pro mote	re cord	scaf fold	spin ster
pros trate	re deem	scep tic	splen did
prov erb	re fer	schoon er	sprin kle
pru dent	re gard	scis sors	squir rel
pud ding	re joice	scram ble	stam mer
pul pit	re lapse	sculp ture	steal thy
pum mel	re main	sea calf	sti fle
pun ish	rem nant	shab by	stock ing
pur chase	ren der	shelter	stran ger
pur pose	re pent	shoul der	strip ling
puz zle	re proach	shudder	stub born
Quad rant	re quest	side board	stu dent
quit tance	re spond	si lence	sub lime
Rab bit	re tard	skim mer	suc ceed
rad ish	re venge	slan der	sud den
rain bow	ri band	slee py	suf fer
ram part	ring let	slip per	sug gest
ran cid	ro mance	sloth ful	sum mit
rap ture	rub bish	slug gish	sup plant
ras cal	Sa cred	smat ter	sur mise
rat tle	saf fron	snap pish	sus pense

WORDS OF TWO SYLLABLES.

Lesson VI.

swal low	un seen	wel come	won der
swin dler	un truth	well bred	wood cock
sym bol	up braid	west ward	wood en
Tal low	ut most	where as	wood land
tam per	Va cant	where in	wool en
tank ard	var nish	wheth er	work man
tar nish	vel lum	whim per	wor ry
ta vern	venge ful	whis per	wor ship
tem per	ver dict	whis tle	wor sted
thatch er	ves try	wick ed	wor thy
thim ble	vil lage	wi den	wo ven
threat en	vin tage	wil ling	wrap per
thun der	vir tue	wil low	wrest ling
tinc ture	vol ley	wind mill	wretch ed
tor ment	vul ture	win dow	wrin kle
trou ble	Wain scot	win dy	wri ter
tum ble	wan der	win ter	writ ten
twen ty	war den	wis dom	Yeo man
Um pire	wasp ish	witch craft	yield ing
un heard	weal thy	with er	yon der
un lock	wea ther	with in	young ster
un mask	web ster	with out	youth ful
un paid	wed ding	wo ful	Zeal ous
un ripe	weigh ty	wo man	zeal ot

READING LESSONS—Lesson 1.

Do you know who God is ?

No one has told me, John.   Who is God?

God is He who made the sun, the moon, the stars, and all you see.

Did he make men?

Yes, He made men, and beasts, and birds, and all that live.

Is God good and kind ?

Yes; He is good, and He does good to all.

In what way is He good to you and me?

He gives us life at first, and He now keeps us from harm by night and by day.

Who gives us our food?

God.   It is He who gives us our food, and clothes, and all the good things we have.

LESSON II.

Does God *think* of us?

Yes : if He did not, how could He take care of us?

And does He think of such a child as I am?

Yes, He thinks of you, to give you food by day, and
to keep you safe when you sleep.

But if He did not, what then?

Then a fire might break out and burn you in your bed,
or a thief might come in and kill you.

Can God *see* us?

Yes, He sees us at all times.

What! can He see us in the night too?

Just as well as in the day.

Does he know what we *do*?

Yes, the least thing we do is known to Him.

And can He hear what we *say* too?

Yes; and he knows even what we *think*.

Why did God make you and me?

He made us that we might know and love Him.

When He is so good to us, we ought to love Him.

LESSON III.

But how can we shew that we love Him?
When we serve Him, then we shew our love to Him.
What is it to serve Him?
It is to do all He bids us.
What does God bid us do?
He says, Love God with all thy heart.
Do not take the name of God in vain.
Keep ho-ly the Lord's-day.
O-bey thy pa-rents.
Do not kill.   Do not swear.
Do not tell a lie.   Do not steal.
Do not wish for what is not thy own.
But if I do these bad things, will God *know* it?
I do not see Him, how then can He see me?
Does he not keep you safe at night?
Yes, you have just told me that He does.
And is He not near you by day to give you food? Yes.

LESSON IV.

Then is He not near you too, to see all you do and hear
all you say?

True; I now see that He must know all.

But will God be an-gry if I do not what he bids me?

Yes, He will in-deed.

And if He be an-gry with me, what then?

That will be worse for you than if all the men in the
world were an-gry with you.

Why?

He can cause you to die, and then send you to hell.

Hell—what is hell?

The place where God sends all who do not love and
o-bey Him.

But I have of-ten done these bad things. What shall
I do?

Beg of God to for-give you for His Son's sake.

LESSON V.

How came you to know all these things?
I have read them in a book.
In a book? What book?
In God's book. Have you not heard of it?
God's book! What book is that?
A book which God gave to men, to teach them all these
    things.
How kind that was. May I read that book?
Yes, when you can read well. It is The **BIBLE**.

A brief Sum of the Gospel, comprehended in the twelve
Articles of the Creed.

1. In God the Fath-er I be-lieve,
2. In Christ al-so, his on-ly Son,
3. Whom a pure Vir-gin did con-ceive,
4. Who died for our re-demp-tion,
5. But he re-viv'd, death lost its sting ;
6. Then heav-en did him with joy re-ceive,
7. Whence he'll re-turn as judge and king.
8. I in the Ho-ly Ghost be-lieve,
9. By whom the church is sanc-ti-fi-ed ;
10. The guilt of sin is par-don'd then ;
11. All shall re-vive that e'er have died ;
12. And life shall ev-er last. Amen.

The Lord is my shep-herd, I shall not want.

Yea, though I walk through the Val-ley of the Shad-ow of Death, I will fear no e-vil, for thou art with me; thy rod and thy staff they comfort me.

O how great is thy good-ness, which thou hast laid up for them that fear thee, and which thou hast wrought for them that trust in thee, even be-fore the sons of men.

Lord, make me to know my end, and the mea-sure of my days, what it is, that I may know how frail I am.

Be-hold thou hast made my days as a hand's breadth, and my age is as noth-ing be-fore thee.

Teach me, O Lord, the way of thy sta-tutes, and I shall keep them to the end.

Thou art good, and do-est good; teach me thy laws.

Thy word have I hid in my heart, that I might not sin a-gainst thee.

PRAYERS AND GRACES.

A Prayer for Morning.

Bles-sed be God for pre-serv-ing me this night past ;
God bless me and keep me from sin and dan-ger this
day fol-low-ing, and give me grace to love and serve
him, and to hon-our and o-bey my fath-er and moth-er,
ac-cord-ing to his com-mand-ments, that I may in-her-
it the king-dom of hea-ven, through Je-sus Christ.
A-men.

A Prayer for Evening.

Bles-sed be God for keep-ing me this day past in
health and safe-ty : O God, for-give me my sins, and
give me grace to do so no more : O God, give me faith
in Christ, and sal-va-tion by him : God bless me, and
keep me, and my fath-er and moth-er, and all my friends,
this night and for ev-er, through Je-sus Christ. A-men.

A Grace before Meat.

Sanc-ti-fy, O Lord, we be-seech thee, these thy good crea-tures, to our use, and us to thy service, through Je-sus Christ our Sa-vi-our.　Amen.　　　　•

A Grace after Meat.

Bles-sed and prais-ed be thy ho-ly name, O God, for these and all thy oth-er bles-sings be-stow-ed up-on us, through Je-sus Christ our Lord.　A-men.

A Prayer for a child before seating himself in Church.

Let the words of my mouth, and the me-di-ta-tions of my heart, be now and ev-er ac-cep-t-a ble in thy sight, O Lord! my strength and my re-deem-er.　A-men.

www.ingramcontent.com/pod-product-compliance
Lightning Source LLC
Chambersburg PA
CBHW031246260626
47169CB00007B/2471